Storming Fort Koopa

Mario crawls past the guard tower and into an open window. He walks slowly down the hall, peering into room after room, but he finds nothing. Fort Koopa seems deserted.

"I guess no one's home," Mario says to himself as he rounds a corner. Then he freezes in his tracks.

He's in the throne room of King Bowser Koopa. The walls are covered with portraits of the evil turtle king. Mario can tell they're pictures of Bowser, because the real Bowser is there in person, too.

Mario has no time to back out of the room. Two massive green arms stretch out menacingly above his head. Bowser's mouth widens into a snaggle-toothed grin.

"Uh-oh," whispers Mario.

What should Mario do next?
It's up to you to make the decisions that will get him through this hair-raising adventure!

Nintendo® Adventure Books:

DOUBLE TROUBLE
LEAPING LIZARDS

Available from ARCHWAY Paperbacks

DOUBLE TROUBLE

By Clyde Bosco

AN ARCHWAY PAPERBACK
Published by POCKET BOOKS

New York   London   Toronto   Sydney   Tokyo   Singapore

To Juana and Kelly
who inspired us to play with power

AN ARCHWAY PAPERBACK *ORIGINAL*

An Archway Paperback published by
POCKET BOOKS, a division of Simon & Schuster
1230 Avenue of the Americas, New York NY 10020

ISBN: 0-671-74112-8

First Archway Paperback Printing June 1991

10 9 8 7 6 5 4 3 2 1

AN ARCHWAY PAPERBACK and colophon are registered trademarks of Simon & Schuster Inc.

Printed in U.S.A.

IL 5+

Creative Media Applications, Inc.
Series developed by Dan Oehlsen, Lary Rosenblatt & Barbara Stewart
Art direction by Fabia Wargin Design
Cover painting by Greg Wray
Puzzle art by Josie Koehne
Edited by Eloise Flood

Special thanks to Ruth Ashby, Lisa Clancy, Paolo Pepe
& George Sinfield

Dear Game Player:

You are about to guide me through a great adventure. As you read this book, you will help me decide where to go and what to do. Whether I succeed or fail is up to you.

At the end of every chapter, you will make choices that determine what happens next. Special puzzles will help you decide what I should do—if you can solve them. The chapters in this book are in a special order. Sometimes you must go backward in order to go forward, if you know what I mean.

Along the way, you'll find many different items to help me with my quest. When you read that I have found something, such as a magnifying glass, you'll see a box like the one below:

> ### *** Mario collects one coin, and he now has the magnifying glass.***
> ### Turn to page 96.

Use page 121 to keep track of the things you collect and to keep score.

Good luck!
Driplessly yours,

Mario

Bzzang! Clang! Bee-bee-beep! It's the emergency alarm! Red warning lights begin to flash. One after another, alarm bells ring throughout the Mario Bros.' house.

"Ooooh," groans Mario, opening one eye. The bedroom he shares with his brother Luigi is almost pitch black, but their plunger-shaped alarm clock glows in the dark. Mario squints at the faint green numbers. "It's three in the morning," he moans. Sitting up, he runs a hand through his thick black hair.

Ahooooghah! Honk! Before Mario has a chance to get out of bed, the alarm goes off a second time. The lights automatically switch on and a pillow on the end of a mechanical arm swings down from the ceiling. It knocks Mario out of the top bunk and onto the floor.

"All right, all right, I'm up," he grumbles, scrambling into his bright red overalls. Grabbing his hat and his waterproof plumber's

1

wristwatch, he charges out of the bedroom and down the hall. He hurries past the supply room, the game room, and the kitchen, and heads into the plumbing workshop to answer the emergency call.

The place is a mess, as usual. A pair of socks hangs among the racks of wrenches and spare copper tubing. On a table, buried under several stale bologna sandwiches, is a broken garbage disposal.

"Definitely have to get this room organized someday," says Mario. "But I'd better answer this call first."

Mario sits down in front of the Mushroom Kingdom Network System, which takes up the eastern wall of the workshop. He shoves a two-day-old plate of ravioli to one side and throws the main power switch.

"Now, let's see what all the fuss is about," he says as he waits for the video screen to come to life.

The Mario Bros.' communication system has come a long way since the day they were first called upon to save the Mushroom Kingdom. Back then, they had to listen for Princess Toadstool's voice ringing through the pipe that leads from her mysterious world to the plumbing shop. Now they rely on an advanced network of computers, radio telescopes, homing pigeons and TV monitors. But, for some reason, today the network doesn't seem to be working.

"Mario . . . *Crackle* . . . quickly!" The voice of Princess Toadstool fades in and out of one speaker. Mario fiddles with several dials, but the video screen is awash with static. "Bring Luigi and a . . . *Buzz*. . . to the palace . . . *Crackle* . . . please hurry!"

"I'm not going to bother trying to get this equipment working," says Mario, getting up from his chair. "It sounds like the princess needs us there on the double!"

Turn to page 4.

3

"Luigi! Wake up!" Mario calls as he runs back into the bedroom.

No one answers.

Mario considers waking his brother with a bucket of cold water. But the last time he did that, Luigi got even by filling Mario's shoes with some of his top secret spaghetti sauce. So Mario leans over the bottom bunk where his brother sleeps and gently pulls back the heavy wool blanket.

The bed is empty!

"That's strange," says Mario, puzzled. "Luigi usually sleeps seventeen hours a day. Why would he be up at this time of night?"

He looks around the bedroom. Everything is in its place—two dressers, a stand-up mirror, their comic book collection—but there's no sign of Luigi.

Mario peers down the hall and notices a faint blue light spilling out of the kitchen door-

4

way. But before he has a chance to investigate, the Mushroom Kingdom alarm begins to ring once more.

Ahoogah! Ahoogah!

"I'm coming, Princess!" shouts Mario. He runs down the hallway and starts to unlock the supply room door. At that moment, the alarm goes off again, louder than ever.

Should Mario look for supplies? Maybe he should find Luigi first. Or maybe he should just head to the Mushroom Kingdom immediately. He'd better decide—quickly!

If you think Mario should search for Luigi, turn to page 100.

If you think Mario should get supplies, turn to page 34.

If you think Mario should head straight to the Mushroom Kingdom, turn to 68.

"All right," announces Mario, looking at GLOM. "It's time for me to take this thing apart and see what makes it tick."

As he approaches the machine, it wheels backward for a few feet. Then the evil contraption abruptly stops. Several parts around its frame begin to grind and turn. With a pop, GLOM coughs out an exact copy of Mario.

"Out of my way, you phony clone," shouts Mario, charging toward GLOM. The fake Mario stands in his way. The two plumbers collide head-on and fall to the floor. Both rub their foreheads in unison and stand up at the same time.

"I'll take care of you first," says Mario. He punches his double on the jaw. At that exact moment, the double punches *him* on the jaw.

"Take that!" Mario shouts as he slaps his twin. The fake Mario's hand flicks out in exactly the same way.

The two Marios punch, slap and kick each other until both collapse on the floor from exhaustion and pass out—at exactly the same time.

Iggy Koopa grabs the real Mario by the straps on his red overalls and drags him back to the maze of mirrors. He leaves the plumber there, asleep on the floor.

A few hours later, Mario wakes. "My beard stubble is getting out of hand," he comments as he looks in one of the mirrors. "Well, the sooner I get this adventure over with, the sooner I can shave." Sighing, he heads toward where he thinks the lab is.

Turn to page 118.

Mario quickly grabs a heavy wooden oar from the deck of the Doom Ship. Just as Roy reaches him, Mario swings the oar.

It hits Roy and snaps like a toothpick.

"Rrrrrooooaaar!" Roy slams into Mario. The plumber is stunned by the blow and before he knows what's happened, Roy is holding him high above his head with both arms.

"About the flowers, and the hospital—I was just kidding, Roy," says Mario meekly.

"Hrrraarrr!" The reptile tosses Mario over the side of the Doom Ship. Mario's flailing hands snatch at a rail that encircles the ship's hull. Saved! He throws one leg over the rail and hauls himself up.

His head is spinning as he tries to stand. Only the narrow metal rail keeps him from falling.

Turn to page 94.

Mario decides to risk the shortcut and climbs down into the ravine.

Zing! Something whizzes over his left shoulder. A blazing chain of fireballs with a small, alligator-like head rockets past him. The air around the plumber instantly gets a few degrees warmer.

"Firesnakes!" Mario shouts. He drops to the ground—just in time to avoid being scorched by a sizzling monster. He pops his head up and risks a quick look around. "If I can only make it to that bush over there, I'll be safe," he tells himself.

A Firesnake zooms over Mario's head and lights up the sky as it makes a sharp U-turn. Along the way, it brushes against the bush, which immediately bursts into flames.

"On second thought, maybe I'll try to reach that cluster of rocks up ahead," says Mario as he dodges the flying flamethrowers.

9

Solve this puzzle to find out what happens next:

Mario would like to avoid as many Firesnakes as possible! Draw a path from the plumber to the rocks. Then add up the number of Firesnakes he passes along the way. If Mario has the Super Mushroom, he has extra power to hop over the blazing monsters, so you can subtract three from your total score.

If Mario passes five or less snakes, turn to page 55.

If Mario passes six to ten snakes, turn to page 97.

If Mario passes eleven or more snakes, turn to page 110.

Bowser steps forward, blocking the doorway. "I've been waiting here for your brother," he snarls. "I heard Luigi was captured and I was looking forward to chewing him into little pieces. He never showed up, but you'll do just fine." The giant turtle moves closer to Mario. "Any last requests?"

"Just one, your slime-ness," says Mario bravely. "I want to know where all these twins are coming from."

Bowser cackles, breathing out a cloud of greenish smoke. "It's all happening right here in this fortress," he crows. "My kid Iggy—the brainy one—put together a machine that makes instant copies of anything it sees. That includes turtles, mushrooms, chickens . . . and even nosy plumbers!

"Anything the machine creates is under Koopa control," Bowser continues, gloating. He paces back and forth. "The way I see it, I'll be running most of the people in the Mushroom Kingdom by next Tuesday."

Mario inches toward the door. Suddenly, Bowser notices what Mario is doing. He scrambles to block the way.

"As I was saying," he growls. "On Tuesday, I'll call a vote and have myself elected Grand Imperial Boss. Then you'll see some changes! I'll get rid of that crummy king and his fungus friends." He blurts out a sour green laugh. "I may keep copies of you and Luigi around, though, just for laughs."

Mario looks around the room for another way out, but with no luck. "Interesting. So where do you keep this machine?" he asks.

"I'm not telling you!" shouts Bowser. "Besides, it wouldn't help you. Your time is up. I'm going to lock you in a room with sixty-four red Koopa Troopas—hah, hah, hah!"

Bowser reaches out a scaly fist to grab Mario. The agile plumber jumps back. Bowser swings a second time, but Mario dodges again. Then Bowser charges. Mario leaps over the turtle king's head and races out the door.

"I'll get you, plumber!" Bowser yells, lumbering after him.

Mario dashes down the hall, searching frantically for clues. "That machine is here someplace," he pants. "But where?"

Ahead of him, a huge marble staircase sweeps up to the second floor of Fort Koopa. A sign on the wall seems to have directions on it—but it's written in Koopanese!

"Swell," Mario mutters. "I left my Koopanese dictionary at home."

His only other choice is to head for the end of the hall. The squishing sound of Bowser's feet grows louder behind him. Bowser is gaining! Which way should Mario go?

Decode this Koopanese message to see which way Mario should go.

• Mario doesn't have a clue—but you do. Use the chart below to learn the letters of the Koopabet.

If you think Mario should go down the hall to look for the machine, turn to page 61.

If you think Mario should look for the machine upstairs, turn to page 18.

"Left," Mario says. He turns left and walks into another glass wall. "Ow," he grumbles, and rubs his bruised nose. He feels his way along until he reaches another turning point.

"You've got to be kidding," he groans. "I think this is where I came in."

Suddenly he hears something. The sound of machinery hums in the background, but Mario can't tell where the sound is coming from. However, there are only two paths.

"Hey," says Mario, "I bet one of these paths will lead me right to Iggy Koopa . . . ."

Solve this puzzle to help decide where Mario should go next:

• Study the picture of Mario, then study all of his reflections below. If you look carefully, you'll notice that some of them are slightly different.

• Cross out all the ones that don't match the Mario pictured at the top. The letters underneath the drawings spell out a message that tells you what Mario should do next.

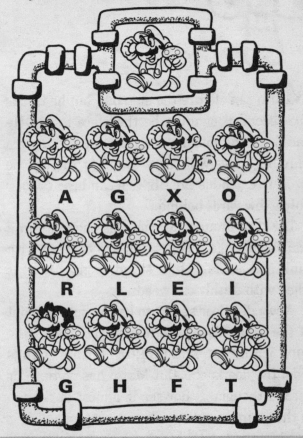

A G X O

R L E I

G H F T

If you think Mario should go left, turn to page 43.

If you think Mario should go right, turn to page 60.

17

Mario can't figure the sign out, but he thinks the second floor must be the place to go. He races up the marble staircase as fast as his plumber's legs will carry him. At the top, he stops to catch his breath. He can hear Bowser only a few yards behind.

Looking around, Mario sees that he's in a waiting lounge. The walls are covered with pink polka-dots. On a stand, a glass bowl is filled with freshly cut weeds.

A wooden door seems to be the only way out of the area. A sign that says "PLEASE KNOCK, WIPE YOUR FEET, AND DO NOT DISTURB" hangs from the doorknob. But Mario has no time for second thoughts. Bowser is almost at the top of the stairs now.

"Trick or treat!" Mario shouts. He throws open the door and charges inside.

Turn to page 95.

Ignoring the Micro-Goombas, Mario makes a desperate dash to the cluster of tubing. "Time to pipe down!" he shouts.

The Para-Goombas are caught off guard. Before they can gather their wits to attack again, Mario dives into a rusty pipe section and rolls himself into a ball. He made it!

"That was close—and kind of gross!" he pants, picking sticky mushrooms from his clothes, mustache and eyelashes.

The giant fungi circle the pipe for a while, waiting for Mario to come out. But Para-Goombas get bored easily. Soon they give up and flap away. Mario stays hidden in the pipe until the last of the flying pests has disappeared.

Sitting in the dark tube, he notices several loose coins scattered about. "Oh, good," he says, gathering them up. "Now I can buy Wooster that computerized feather duster he's been asking for."

After a few minutes, Mario heads back to check out the huge, dark object, still hovering in the sky.

*** Mario collects 16 coins ***
Turn to page 51.

"Toad could be just about anywhere," Mario sighs, as he looks out across the Mushroom Kingdom countryside. But the plumber doesn't get much time to think about the places he could go to look for Toad. Less than five minutes from the palace, he hears Toad's squeaky voice. And it's coming from the very center of an enormous Piranha Patch!

"Oh no," says Mario. He gazes into the field of swirling, snarling green plants. "These overgrown flytraps are bad news."

"Save me!" cries Toad.

Mario can see a white dot in the middle of the moving green field. "I'm on my way!" he calls, and begins to make his way through the vicious plants.

Turn to page 90.

Mario slips between Iggy and GLOM and runs to the other side of the room. He grabs test tubes, books, chairs—anything he can find—and hurls them at the slowly advancing machine. None of it does any damage.

GLOM backs Mario up against the green double doors that lead back to the hall of mirrors. "Give it up, Mario. You're finished!" calls Iggy Koopa.

Desperately, Mario dives through the doors and tries to hold them shut. "Can't ... hold ... them ... much ... longer," he grunts as GLOM slowly forces the doors open.

Then, a smile forms on Mario's lips. He lets go of the doors and stands to one side.

"We're open. Please come in!" he calls, as GLOM pushes its way into the corridor.

The giant machine rolls into the mirrored hallway and begins to circle in search of Mario. As it turns, it catches a glimpse of its own bizarre reflection in one of the mirrors.

It stops.

Slowly, the screens and light bulbs that pepper the sides of the hideous machine begin to flash, and a high-pitched whine fills the air. There's a bright flash. When the smoke clears, Mario is pleased to see that GLOM has created an exact duplicate of itself!

The two machines begin to examine each other, sniffing each other's TV screens and buttons. A moment later, there's another small explosion. This time, when the dust settles, there are four duplicating machines.

Mario crouches behind one of the double doors and watches as the number of GLOMs goes from 128, to 256, to 512. The machines have long since crowded out of the hallway. Now they fill the lab from wall to wall.

"Stop! Wait! You're ruining everything!" Iggy shrieks as the four-thousandth GLOM is coughed into existence.

When there are about ten thousand of them, some of the machines begin to explode.

"Time to make like a headache and start splitting!" says Mario, picking his way through channels of broken mirror frames. By the time he reaches the stairs, huge clusters of duplicating machines are starting to self-destruct. He races down the hallway and dives out the first open window he finds. He rolls to the bottom of the hill as Fort Koopa crumbles in an explosion of smoke, lightning and strange machine parts.

Later, when the dust begins to settle, Mario thinks he sees three large, rounded shapes scurry from the wreckage and slither away, but he can't be certain.

Turn to page 69.

"You go outside. I'll meet you there," Mario says, smiling. The other plumber nods and heads out the side door of the shop.

". . . When cows can fly," Mario adds as soon as he's alone. "Either Luigi is acting stranger than usual, or that's some kind of impostor. He didn't make one dumb joke and he went all the way across the room without bouncing up and down like a goofball.

"Besides," Mario continues, "we can't waste time working on an invention while the princess is in trouble. Something strange is going on, and I'll bet it has to do with the weird way Luigi is acting."

Mario runs to the supply room and grabs a Super Mushroom for extra power in an emergency. Then he hurries back to the workshop.

*** Mario now has the Super Mushroom. ***
Turn to page 68.

Mario decides to check out the Mushroom Kingdom before heading to the palace. "A quick peek is always a good idea," he says to himself as he bounces down the road.

Mario thinks the Mushroom Kingdom is the most beautiful place he's ever seen. It's full of roaring waterfalls, brilliant rainbows, and clear, sparkling ponds. The weather is nearly always sunny and warm. And with all the pipe passageways, underground caverns, and hidden treasures Mario keeps discovering, there are endless opportunities for adventure.

Of course, even beautiful places have their problems. When he travels to the Mushroom Kingdom, Mario's almost certain to run into some unfriendly creatures. Tweeter birds always try to land on his head. Masked Snifits often sting him with pointy little bullets. If he tries to have a picnic, giant Hoopster bugs are almost certain to carry away half of the food.

But Mario is a professional creature-dodger as well as a master plumber. Even though there seem to be twice as many pests as usual, he hops and skips over pairs of Shyguys, Fryguys and Clawgrips with the grace of a fine ballet dancer—or at least of a mediocre football player.

Mario counts the creatures as he walks. "Something is definitely wrong here," he says. "I'm seeing everything twice!"

As he tries to figure out what direction the creatures are coming from, Mario notices two separate shapes approaching in the sky. One seems to be a flock of small creatures. The other is harder to see, but it looks like one huge, shadowy form.

If you think Mario should head toward the flock of small creatures, turn to page 31.

If you think Mario should head toward the giant shadow, turn to page 51.

The first boomerang sails over Mario's head, missing him by almost a yard. "Is that the best you can do?" he taunts. He turns and sneers at the monstrous turtle twins.

But Mario has forgotten that these weapons return. When the boomerang circles and bashes him on the back of the head, he has no idea what hit him. His knees buckle and he falls.

The Boomerang Brothers lumber up to where Mario is lying out cold.

"Not bad," remarks one of the turtles, picking Mario up by a leg. He tosses the plumber into a sack of old orange peels and other things he has picked up in his travels. Then he slings the sack over his shoulder.

The second turtle yawns. "I'm tired."

"Me too," says his brother. "Let's go home and make a nice pot of plumber soup."

GAME OVER!

Swish! *Swish!* The cloud of boomerangs sails over Mario's head. They miss denting his cap—not to mention his skull—by the narrowest of margins.

When he sees the deadly swarm begin to turn around, the plumber hits the dirt until the boomerangs whoosh past him once more. Then he gets up and makes a frantic dash away from the giant turtles.

As powerful, terrible, and truly awful as they are, the Boomerang Brothers aren't very fast. Soon they're choking on Mario's dust.

"I'll deal with those two goons later," Mario pants, tearing down the road to Fort Koopa. "Maybe in another adventure."

When he reaches the massive stone fortress, Mario peeps through the castle's dingy windows. He can see lights on in almost every room, but there's no sign of life. Quietly, he walks inside and begins to explore the filthy rooms.

Just when he's decided the castle is turtle-free, he rounds a corner and runs smack into a large, leathery leg.

"Hello, Lunch," croaks a deep voice.

Mario looks up silently. Bad news! He's standing at the feet of none other than Bowser Koopa, king of the turtles.

Turn to page 12.

16

Mario heads for the cloud of creatures. As he gets close, they begin to swirl about in the sky. Suddenly, the entire flock swoops down on him.

It's a swarm of Para-Goombas! Not all mushrooms in the kingdom are nice—and these brown flying fungi are some of the worst. *Plop! Plop! Plop!* They shower him with tiny, sticky baby mushrooms as they sail by.

"Yuck!" exclaims Mario, stumbling along the road. Micro-Goombas cling to his mustache. "I've got to find cover, or I'll be smothered."

The giant winged mushrooms reverse course and sail past Mario again, pelting him. He pulls away fistfuls of sticky fungus. But the Para-Goombas bomb him a third time.

It's getting hard for Mario to see. As he wipes off the little pests, two of the large fungi settle on a wall, licking their pulpy lips.

"These guys are ready to order, and it looks like I'm the main course," says Mario.

Up ahead is a pile of rusty pipes. Mario thinks he'll be able to hide in them. But if he doesn't get rid of those sticky little mushrooms first, he might not make it!

Solve this puzzle to help decide what Mario should do:

• Thirteen flying pests that Mario wants to avoid are hidden in this word search. Words go up, down, forward and backward. Use the word list for help. Circle them all, and the left-over letters will tell you what Mario should do.

TWEETER   **PARA-GOOMBA**   **PHANTO**

BEEZO   **HOT FOOT**   **CHEEP CHEEP**

ALBATOSS   **THWOMP**   **FRYGUY**

PIDGIT   **BOO**   **PARA-BEETLE**

           NINJI

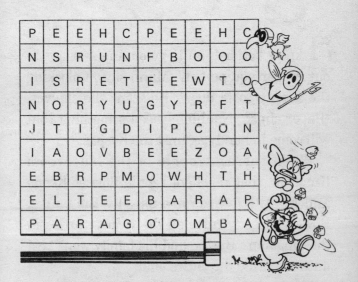

P	E	E	H	C	P	E	E	H	C
N	S	R	U	N	F	B	O	O	O
I	S	R	E	T	E	E	W	T	O
N	O	R	Y	U	G	Y	R	F	T
J	T	I	G	D	I	P	C	O	N
I	A	O	V	B	E	E	Z	O	A
E	B	R	P	M	O	W	H	T	H
E	L	T	E	E	B	A	R	A	P
P	A	R	A	G	O	O	M	B	A

If you think Mario should stop and clear away the Micro-Goombas, turn to page 104.

If you think Mario should ignore the Micro-Goombas and run for cover, go to page 19.

"I know better than to go on a mission without proper equipment," Mario says, unlocking the supply room door. He scans the shelves. "Paper clips? Naahh. I need something that will come in handy against the Koopas."

When there's trouble in the Mushroom Kingdom, that repellent reptile Bowser Koopa and his turtle kids are usually the cause. Bowser already rules all the vicious turtles in the kingdom. But he and his family won't rest until they rule the entire land.

Mario thinks of the time Bowser tried to carry the kingdom's doorknobs away in a hot air balloon. "It's a good thing someone had a pea shooter with him that day," he says.

Unfortunately, Mario has no idea what's going on at the palace now. He walks through the maze-like shelves of plumbing tools, cooking utensils and inflatable beach toys.

"Should I bring some Swiss cheese? A bicycle pump? If the Koopas are up to their old tricks again, what will I need to stop them this time?" he wonders.

Solve this puzzle to see what equipment Mario takes with him to the Mushroom Kingdom.

• Choose one path for Mario and follow it until he reaches an object. That item is the one Mario takes.

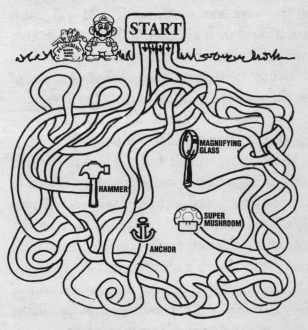

Then turn to page 68.

"**T**his is my Giant Likeness Outputting Machine," Iggy says. He giggles. "I call it GLOM for short. It took months to build, but all the work was worth it. GLOM will finish you off and then get back to business—taking over the Mushroom Kingdom."

As Iggy twitters on, Mario has time to examine the machine. GLOM is truly frightening to look at, even for Mario, who has seen some pretty scary things inside drain pipes.

More than ten feet tall, GLOM is covered with giant electronic eyeballs and hundreds of tiny television sets, each displaying a different 1960's monster movie. It crawls across the floor on a combination of wheels, feet, and tank treads that leave a slime trail behind them. GLOM stops for a moment and spits a pair of Koopa Troopas out of a funnel at its top. Then it rolls next to Iggy and comes to a halt.

"Beautiful, isn't it?" asks the turtle prince.

He gestures to a bank of TV screens on one of the walls. "I've hidden cameras all over the Mushroom Kingdom and beyond," he explains. "With the information they send back, GLOM can scoop up sand from our yard and make it into a perfect double of anyone. That's how I copied the king. I would have gotten the princess, Toad and Wooster too, if that finicky fungus hadn't ruined my plan by watering one of my cameras."

On one of the flickering screens, Mario sees Luigi bouncing cheerfully around their shop at home, tinkering with a stopped-up sink.

Iggy notices Luigi, too. "Hey!" the turtle shouts, stamping his lumpy green foot. "I put a double in your brother's place, but it can't be that guy. He's singing! Doubles don't sing. That's the real thing. Something went wrong."

Mario laughs. "It looks like Luigi clobbered your clone."

"Well, I've still got you. GLOM! Get the plumber!" Iggy shouts, pointing at Mario.

The machine slowly grinds toward Mario. Suddenly it reaches out one of its mechanical arms and tries to grab him. But Mario is too quick to be caught that way. He ducks as the metal claw swings over his head. He dashes behind GLOM and waits for it to turn around.

The machine turns. Mario edges backward, trying to buy time and avoid sure destruction. He is so distracted by the machine that he loses track of Iggy. The sneaky turtle sticks out his foot and trips Mario. Our hero stumbles into a corner and falls down, hitting his head yet again.

GLOM closes in. "Crush him!" Iggy yells.

Mario scrambles to his feet, but he's trapped.

"I guess this is it," he mutters. He looks around the lab. To his left is Iggy, rubbing his wart-covered hands and cackling with glee. To his right, Mario can see the green doors that lead back into the maze of mirrors. Straight ahead, GLOM crawls steadily toward him.

Solve this puzzle for a hint:

- Draw a straight line from Iggy to GLOM.
- Draw a straight line from Iggy to the exit.
- Draw a straight line from the exit to Glom.
- Draw a straight line from Mario to the exit.
- Study the picture. The leftover letters spell out some advice for Mario.

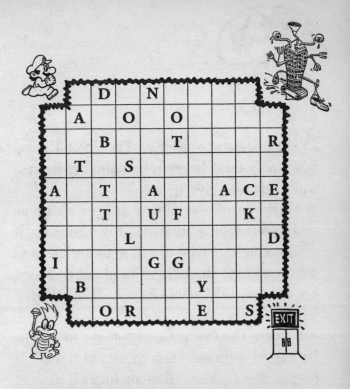

If you think Mario should go after Iggy Koopa, turn to page 92.

If you think Mario should attack GLOM, turn to page 6.

If you think Mario should run away, turn to page 22.

Mario decides to go for it. The Chain Chomp is the only thing between him and the fortress walls. He can't give up now.

Mario decides to play a dangerous game with the snapping monster. If he can make it mad enough, maybe it will get careless and Mario will get through. The plumber waves his arms at the Chain Chomp. "Hey, Baldy!" he yells.

Clack! The Chain Chomp snaps at Mario. Its jagged teeth miss him by almost a foot. It lunges again. Mario flattens himself against the ground, and the Chain Chomp whizzes by.

Now it's really mad! When it rears and growls, Mario ducks under its nose and races for the wall.

"And awa-a-a-y we go!" he yells, as the Chain Chomp swings in for one last bite.

Solve this puzzle to find out what happens next:

• Which route should Mario take to reach the top of the wall safely? Look carefully at the length of each Chain Chomp's chain.

If you think Mario should take route A, turn to page 56.

If you think Mario should take route B, turn to page 113.

"Let's do it," says Mario, as he spins the great wooden steering wheel. He pilots the Doom Ship back to the entrance of the Mushroom Kingdom. There, the two plumbers climb down from the ship and crawl into the main pipe. Within minutes, they are back at their plumbing shop in Brooklyn.

"Oh Mister Impostor, come out, come out wherever you are," sings Mario, sauntering into the workshop.

Luigi's evil twin pokes his head around the corner to find out what's going on. By the time the slow-witted duplicate decides to run, it's too late. Mario has blocked the door.

"Will all sensitive and delicate people please leave the auditorium at this time," announces Luigi. "The Super Mario Bros. are back in town."

Turn to page 49.

"Let's try this way." Mario turns left, going down a series of mirrored halls. The machine noises grow louder. At last, he turns a corner and steps into a plain cement hall.

"I'm free!" he cries. "But I'll miss those guys in the mirror. They were so good looking!"

Mario marches down the hall and pushes open a set of green doors. He steps into a weird laboratory. On the walls are huge spools of wire. Lightbulbs of every color and size flash on control panels. The floor is strewn with test tubes, gears, and—of course—bags of old garbage. Facing Mario is Iggy Koopa.

"Hmm," says Iggy. "I didn't think you'd get through my maze. But since you're here, I'd like you to meet my new creation." He presses a button on a remote control device and a giant machine rolls into the room.

Turn to page 36.

"*Rrroaarr!*" Roy Koopa bellows, charging toward Mario in a blind rage.

Mario calmly steps aside and watches as the awful turtle hurls himself through the guard rail and over the side of the ship. "Oh, nooo . . ." Roy wails. He's heading straight for a patch of snapping black Muncher plants!

"I always knew Roy was going to be a dropout," Mario remarks.

He picks up some shiny coins that are scattered on the planks of the Doom Ship. "This is good," he says. "Now I'll be able to buy the King that gold-plated mustache brush he wanted for his birthday."

"Mmph!" says Luigi, still tied to the mast behind the steering wheel.

Mario unties his brother, who begins to run frantically about the deck.

"Hurry, hurry!" he shouts. "We've got to stop the Koopas while we still have time!"

"Hold on a minute," says Mario. "Would you mind telling me how you got here in the first place?"

"The Koopas grabbed me while I was sleeping," explains Luigi. "They tied me up and left a phony me in my place. I don't know how they're doing it, Mario, but the Koopas are making copies of everybody!" He begins to climb over the rail of the Doom Ship. "I've got to get home and stop that impostor," he calls. "The universe isn't big enough for two Luigis. Are you coming?"

Decode this secret message to get a clue to help decide what Mario should do.

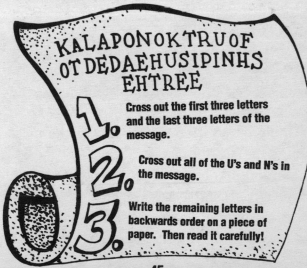

KALAPONOKTRUOF
OTDEDAEHUSIPINHS
EHTREE

1. Cross out the first three letters and the last three letters of the message.

2. Cross out all of the U's and N's in the message.

3. Write the remaining letters in backwards order on a piece of paper. Then read it carefully!

*** Mario collects 11 coins. ***

If you think Mario should go home
with Luigi, turn to page 42.

If you think he should stay behind and
ride with the Doom Ship, turn to page 111.

23

Mario rushes headlong down one, then another, then another flight of stairs. He hears Iggy squishing ahead of him the whole way down. But when he finally reaches the bottom, Iggy is nowhere in sight. The place is silent.

Then, out of the corner of his eye, Mario sees someone move.

"Aha!" he shouts, as he spins around. But instead of Iggy, Mario finds himself face-to-face with a handsome plumber in red overalls.

His first thought is, "This doubles thing has gone too far." Then suddenly, he realizes he's looking at his reflection in a mirror. "Gee," he says. "I need a shave."

As he looks away from the familiar figure, he spots a glass door next to the mirror. Through it he can see a long glass hall lined with rows and rows of mirrors. He opens the door and enters. Behind him, the door swings shut with an ominous click.

Mario shrugs. "Oh well, I wasn't planning to turn back anyway," he says. He walks down the hall into the maze of mirrors.

Turn to page 108.

24

There are a handful of creatures in the Mushroom Kingdom more powerful than either of the Super Mario Bros. But there are almost none who could defeat both of them at once—especially when they're in Brooklyn!

"I'd say we've got the home court advantage, little brother," says Mario, grabbing a plunger from a rack of plumbing tools.

"You are so right," says Luigi, rolling up his sleeves. "Let's make haste and waste this attractive but evil intruder."

The plumbers surround the phony Luigi. Mario bops him on the head with the plunger while Luigi delivers a Double-Tornado belly punch. Their opponent collapses.

Luigi runs to the kitchen and returns with a lukewarm pot of his top secret spaghetti sauce. He pours it over the unlucky impostor. "That should hold him for a while," he says, licking his fingers.

But when the sauce hits the fake Luigi, he begins to melt! The brothers watch in astonishment as the impostor dissolves into a puddle of orange mush.

Mario hurries to the supply room. A moment later he comes back into the workshop with a magnifying glass. "Now, what have we here?" he muses as he inspects the soggy mess on the floor. "Tomato sauce . . . and something else. I can't tell what it is." He tucks the magnifying glass into one of his pockets. "This may come in handy later."

Mario turns to face Luigi. "You wait here in case there are any more messages from the palace. I'm heading there now." He bends to pick up some coins that the fake Luigi dropped during the battle. "I'll buy some comic books with these," he decides. "I hear there are some great new comics featuring two extremely brave and handsome plumbers from Brooklyn." Then he dives into the central pipe.

Mario's back in the Mushroom Kingdom.

*** Mario collects 9 coins, and he now has the magnifying glass. ***

Turn to page 79.

Mario walks toward the solitary giant shadow in the sky. As he gets closer to the floating object, its features become frightfully clear. It's the Doom Ship—the Koopa family's floating battleship and number one secret weapon. It looks very much like an ancient sailing ship, except that it's covered with propellers, bubbling slime spouters, and deadly flame-throwing Koopa cannons. The evil craft is hovering above a bed of snapping black Muncher plants.

"The Doom Ship!" says Mario excitedly. "I knew that dark ark was involved in this business somehow."

Standing at the wheel, searching the landscape with a telescope, is an enormous armored turtle in bright pink sunglasses. It's Roy Koopa, the meanest of the seven Koopa kids. Roy and Mario spot each other in the same instant.

"Yoo-hoo! Roy! Come down here for a

minute," calls Mario. "I've got a few things I'd like to ask you."

"Not on your life, plungerface!" yells Roy. He spins the Doom Ship's great wooden steering wheel. Slowly, the boat turns to the east and begins to drift away.

"Oh no you don't!" Mario dashes after the floating warship. He tries to grab one of the many cables and ropes trailing below the craft, but they're just out of reach.

"Bon voyage!" shouts Roy Koopa.

The Doom Ship starts to rise into the sky. There's plenty more to see in the Mushroom Kingdom. But if Mario is going to try to board the boat, the time is now!

If Mario has the anchor from the supply room, turn to page 105.

If you think Mario should try to jump and reach the Doom Ship, turn to page 87.

If you think Mario should let the Doom Ship go and continue to explore the Mushroom Kingdom, turn to page 58.

"**N**ow we have two contenders for the throne!"

Princess Toadstool leads Mario up to the front of the room, where two identical kings are taking turns pushing each other off the big gold throne. Each is wearing a purple robe and an onion-shaped crown. Wooster, the royal mushroom assistant, is there too, wringing his hands. His usually spotless apron is covered with dirt. He looks as if he hasn't slept for days.

"You've got to help us, Mario!" wails the tall mushroom. "I've been so busy trying to clean up after two kings, I haven't even had time to wind the royal cuckoo clocks!"

"Frankly, your Highness," Mario whispers to the princess, "it could be worse. I've never seen the king actually do anything anyway."

"It's the principle of the thing!" snaps the princess. "Every kingdom needs a king, and there can only be one king in every castle, and we've got two—so . . . help!"

"I'll do what I can," Mario promises.

Just then he notices that Toad, the royal mushroom retainer, is not around. "Where's Toad?" he asks.

"He went out to find a magnifying glass," answers Wooster. "He thought it might help us discover who the real king is."

"Great idea," says one of the two kings.

"I was just about to say that!" cries the other one.

"I wonder whether I have a magnifying glass with me," says Mario. He starts to check his pockets.

*** Check your notes to see what equipment Mario is carrying to decide what happens next. ***

If Mario has a magnifying glass, turn to page 64.

If Mario does not have a magnifying glass, turn to page 116.

STOP! It's impossible to get that result. Go back to the page you just read and try again!

Snap! The Chain Chomp sinks its teeth into the tip of Mario's shoe. It rips away a small piece of leather, but Mario reaches the top of the wall and climbs to safety. He mops his forehead. Then he sits down and pulls off his shredded shoe.

"One, two, three, four, five . . . everybody's still here," says Mario, counting the toes on his bare foot.

"Hraaar," growls the Chain Chomp as it settles down to munch on the tasty piece of shoe leather.

Mario walks along the top of the wall until he reaches the front of the fortress. On his way, he reaches up and knocks down a fistful of coins from an overhead ledge. Then he leaps onto a catwalk and crawls past the guard tower and into an open window.

"This must be Fort Koopa, all right," Mario says. He makes a face. "The windows are filthy."

He walks slowly down the hall, peering into room after room, but he finds nothing. Other than the occasional pitter-patter of cockroach feet, the entire wing of the building is silent. The rooms contain only enormous piles of dust.

"I guess no one's home," Mario says to himself as he rounds the next corner. Then he freezes in his tracks.

He's standing in the throne room of King Bowser Koopa. The walls are covered with several hundred portraits of the evil turtle king. It's easy for Mario to tell that they're pictures of Bowser, because the real Bowser is standing there in person.

Mario has no time to back out of the room. Two massive green arms stretch out menacingly above his head. Bowser's mouth widens into a snaggletoothed grin.

"Uh-oh," whispers Mario.

*** Mario collects 12 coins. ***
Turn to page 12.

Turn to page 12.

Mario tramps on through the Mushroom Kingdom, deep in thought, hopping over pairs of monsters that come at him from every direction. Suddenly he looks up and sees a tangle of snapping, snarling, leafy green monsters ahead. He's at the edge of an enormous field of Piranha plants.

"Help!" cries a squeaky voice from somewhere deep within the Piranha Patch.

"Toad? Is that you?" calls Mario.

A small white head bobs up and down in the very center of the field. It's Toad, the royal mushroom retainer.

"How did you get here?" Mario asks.

"There are two of almost everyone in the kingdom, including the king," Toad says. "I went to find a magnifying glass, but on my way back I got trapped in this field. A turtle with a mustache and glasses told me it was a short cut."

A turtle! It was probably one of the Koopa kids in disguise, but Mario has no time to worry about that right now.

"Hang on, little buddy," he calls, and charges into the thicket of vicious plants.

Turn to page 90.

30

"I guess I'll go right," Mario decides. He bounds into the right-hand fork. "Now we're getting someplace," he says, heading down a new mirrored corridor.

Wham! He walks into another glass wall and falls down. For a few minutes, he sits there, stunned. Then he picks himself up and looks around. He has a choice to make once again, left or right.

"Okay, it's time to get serious," Mario says, reaching into his back pocket. He takes out his lucky penny and tosses it into the air. "Heads I go left, tails I go right. It's simple! When in doubt, let Abe Lincoln figure it out . . . . "

Flip a penny to decide where Mario should go next:

HEADS, turn to page 118.
TAILS, turn to page 108.

Mario decides the long, dingy hallway is the way to go. He races down to the end and darts around a corner. "I need someone who'll lead me to that machine," he says to himself.

Just then, Iggy Koopa waddles past. Bowser's homely, purple-haired son doesn't notice Mario, and continues on his way.

"That's what I call service," murmurs Mario. He falls into step behind Iggy.

They wind through the filthy halls of Fort Koopa, past battle trophies, statues, paintings of ancient Koopa rulers, and bags of garbage that no one has bothered to throw out for centuries. The stench is incredible. But gradually Mario begins to relax. Clearly, Iggy has no idea that he's being followed.

They plod onward, past Bowser's prized rotten vegetable collection. When Iggy turns the next corner, Mario bumps into a statue of Genghis Koopa. It wobbles for a few moments that seem like hours. Mario holds his breath. Will it fall? Won't it?

It falls. With a crash, it hits the floor and shatters into a thousand pieces.

"Eeep!" Iggy cries, as he whirls and spots Mario.

"Eeep," squeaks a mouse that used to live inside the statue. The mouse scurries down the hall and out of sight.

Never one to face a fair fight, Iggy dashes through a doorway by a sign that says "BASE- MENT—IN CASE OF FLOOD, DO NOT ENTER."

"Not so fast, Ig!" Mario calls. He races after Iggy, down a flight of dimly lit stairs.

Solve this puzzle to find out where Mario is headed:

• Mario steps on the first step—the one with a "Q" on it. Cross it out.

• Decide if Mario should touch every other step, every third step, or every fourth step. Cross out the letters on the steps that Mario touches.

• If you got the pattern right, a message will appear. The leftover letters spell where Mario is going.

Turn to page 47.

Magnifying glass in hand, Mario marches up to the throne. Finally, he thinks, a chance to find out what this trouble is all about.

"All right, everyone," he calls, holding up the glass. "Maybe I can straighten things out."

Wooster, the royal assistant, nudges one of the kings toward the plumber. Mario holds the glass in front of the royal nose. "Hmm," he says as he studies the king.

"What is it? What do you see?" asks Wooster impatiently.

"I see . . . a nose," announces Mario. He takes off his cap and scratches his head. Both kings shrug their shoulders.

"Great!" says Princess Toadstool. "Any more brilliant deductions, Mr. Detective?"

"Don't rush me," answers Mario. "Let me take a look at His Majesty Number Two."

Wooster leads the second king to Mario, who holds the glass up to the second regal nose.

But when Mario sees it magnified, it doesn't look like a king's nose at all. It looks more like a sand dune. In fact, up close, no part of this monarch looks like a king. He's made entirely of sand!

"Aha! Here's your impostor," Mario says. "Take him away!"

"I told you I'm me," says the real king.

"I told you I'm me," shouts the impostor as the royal mushroom guards haul him away.

No one says anything as he's dragged from the room. The doors slam behind him. The real king gazes after his double sadly.

"Don't worry," says Wooster. "We have a special home for people who try to impersonate the royal family. He'll have fun." He runs one finger along an arm of the king's throne and inspects the dust buildup. "Of course, it isn't very tidy there," he adds.

"So, what should we do now?" asks Princess Toadstool. "We can't possibly check every set of twins in the kingdom. New ones are showing up every minute."

"No, we've got to get to the root of this problem," Mario agrees, dropping the magnifying glass into his overalls pocket. "The impostor was made of sand, right?"

"Right," answers the princess.

"And where are there tons and tons of sand?" asks Mario.

"The Koopahari Desert," answers Wooster, shuddering. "Frightfully dusty place."

"And what else is in the Koopahari Desert?" continues Mario.

"Fort Koopa!" everyone shouts.

"I'm on my way," Mario declares. He bounces down the hall. "I'll have this double trouble taken care of in no time at all."

"Hooray!" the king shouts.

"Make it snappy," adds the princess.

"And please don't track sand into the palace when you come back," Wooster begs.

Solve this puzzle to find out what could be waiting for Mario in the Koopahari Desert:

• Study this grid and then look at the list at the top of the next page.

• For each entry on the list, match the numbers on the side with the letters along the top. Cross out the corresponding space.

• The letters in the leftover boxes will spell out something Mario will find in the Koopahari Desert.

B2, A1, C3, E2, D5, B6, C1, E3, C4, D4, D2, C5,
E1, A3, C2, E6

	A	B	C	D	E
1	S	T	OP	HE	LP
2	B	OB	O	N	O
3	GL	OO	PU	M	P
4	E	RA	NG	BA	NG
5	B	R	IN	KS	O
6	TH	IP	E	RS	KY

Turn to page 75.

33

"Geronimo!" yells Mario. "It's time to save the Mushroom Kingdom." He dives into the central pipe in the middle of the workshop and tumbles down into darkness. "You know," he mutters to himself, "no matter how often I go to the Mushroom Kingdom, I still hate this part."

He falls through the pipe for hundreds of feet, or maybe hundreds of miles—he can't tell. Then, suddenly, he shoots out the other end and drops into a tuft of spongy grass.

Mario gets up and looks around. High overhead, brick platforms and clusters of metal boxes hang mysteriously suspended from the sky. Rows of bright flowers and polka-dot mushrooms spread out in every direction.

Once again, Mario is at the entrance to the Mushroom Kingdom, the magical land that he and Luigi have vowed to protect.

Turn to page 102.

34

Mario wanders through the wreckage of the once-mighty fortress, picking up great piles of coins scattered among the ruins. "Tee-rrific," he says. "Now I can buy the princess that stainless steel surfboard she's been asking for."

When there are no more coins to be found, Mario brushes the dust from his overalls and bounces off to the palace. As he travels through the Mushroom Kingdom, he can tell that there are already fewer doubles than there were a few hours ago. A light breeze is blowing, and a great many piles of sand are scattered about the countryside.

Finally Mario reaches the palace. He makes his way up the stairs and is about to enter through the royal double doors when he notices the time on his waterproof plumber's wristwatch.

"What?! I've only been out of bed for fifteen minutes?" he asks in disbelief. Then he realizes that he's been awake for more than twenty-four hours.

"I'll tell the princess all about my adventure . . . tomorrow!" he says. He stumbles away from the palace to the kingdom's entrance, climbs the central pipe, and drags himself home. Finally he collapses into his favorite armchair for a three-day nap.

*** Mario collects 200 Coins. ***
You win!
The kingdom has been saved!
GAME OVER!

Luigi leads his brother through the kitchen and out the side door of the plumbing shop. Behind the shop is an alley full of spare parts and strange-looking machines.

"Try this on, please," he mumbles, handing Mario a shiny metal vest. "I'll show you what it can do." A dozen metal cables are connected to the vest. They dangle from the sky above the dark alley. Mario looks up, but it's impossible to see where the cables come from.

The whole thing seems a little strange to him, but then Luigi has always been a bit strange, Mario thinks. He sticks his arms into the vest and begins to fasten the buckles on its front. Then he stops short.

Did Luigi say "Please?" That's something new. Well, maybe it's just because he's tired—after all, he got only twelve hours of sleep today. Mario shrugs and continues to fasten the shiny metal garment.

Luigi waits for his brother to finish. Then he turns slowly and pulls down on a lever sticking out of one of the strange machines. "Goodbye," he says calmly.

Instantly, the cables begin to snake up into the night sky, taking Mario along with them. "Whoa!" he shouts, but he can't do a thing about it. In seconds, Mario is several hundred feet above the ground.

As he comes to a halt, high in the air, Mario sees a dark, familiar object floating towards him. It's the Doom Ship, the evil Koopa family's flying battle boat! Its propellers hum busily and its heavy iron cannons stand ready on the wooden prow.

Mario struggles to break loose, but the cables hold him tightly. He can see an armored turtle in bright pink sunglasses standing on the poop deck as the Doom Ship approaches. He recognizes Roy Koopa—Bowser's son, and one of the rottenest reptiles in the Mushroom Kingdom.

"Drip ahoy!" calls Roy. He reaches out and scoops Mario up into a large net.

Turn to page 85.

Suddenly, Mario remembers that he's been carrying a hammer around with him all day long. "I guess those knocks on the head have dulled my memory," he thinks.

He reaches into his overalls in search of the hammer. "Yes!" he shouts, taking the tool from a pocket. "I knew there was a reason I brought this along." He swings the hammer at the glass panel in front of him. "When in doubt, break something!"

The wall shatters. Mario leaps through the broken glass. "That was fun," he says, and begins to smash a trail through the maze of mirrors, panel by panel.

After about twenty panels, he breaks into a strange, brightly lit room—Iggy Koopa's laboratory! On the walls are huge spools of wire. Lightbulbs of every color and size flash on control panels. The floor is cluttered with test tubes, gears, and—of course—bags of old garbage. In the center of the room, facing Mario, is Iggy himself.

"Well look who's here," says Iggy. "I really didn't think you'd be able to get through my maze. But as long as you've decided to drop by, I'd like to introduce you to one of my creations." He presses a button on a remote control device and a giant machine rolls slowly into the room.

Turn to page 36.

As soon as Mario crosses into the Koopahari Desert, the red brick road ends abruptly. So do the grassy hills, the brooks, and everything else in the Mushroom Kingdom that's lush and colorful. An endless expanse of yellow sand stretches out before Mario. Dunes, crags, and rocky outcroppings dot the landscape. The only plants are a few withered cacti.

However, there's definitely no shortage of living things. "Just as I thought," Mario says, dodging a pair of masked Shyguys that waddle past. "The doubles problem is even worse here than at the palace. Enemies are everywhere, in sets of two, four, and even eight. I've got to put a stop to this quickly, or we'll be knee-deep in creeps!"

In the distance, Mario can see the faint outline of Fort Koopa. A winding road leading to it has been worn in the sand by thousands of feet. But a sign in the shape of a paw standing by the side of the road reads "SHORTCUT TO FORT KOOPA — NOT FOR THE SQUEAMISH." A black-nailed finger points to a rocky ravine just south of where Mario is standing.

"Hmmm," Mario muses. "Something tells me neither of these trails will be a picnic."

Solve this puzzle for a clue about what's ahead:

• Follow the path that leads from Mario to Fort Koopa. Read the letters as you go. They'll tell you something about the short cut through the ravine.

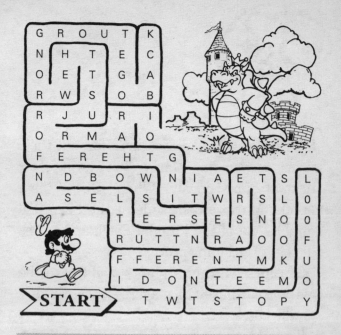

If you think Mario should take the main road to Fort Koopa, turn to page 81.

If you think Mario should follow the shortcut into the ravine, turn to page 9.

The horrible green creatures fan out their leaves, surrounding Mario. They swing their sticks at him viciously. Whap! One of them smacks Mario on the side of the head. He stumbles out of the Piranha Patch and passes out cold. The inning is over.

Of course, Piranha plants could never be really great baseball players—they couldn't run the bases.

When Mario wakes, he staggers back to the entrance to the Mushroom Kingdom. But his whacking has made him forget everything that has happened in the last two hours!

Turn to page 102.

Mario decides he'd better talk to the princess before doing anything else. So he scampers up the path that leads to the palace.

Along the way, and on into the distance in every direction, the landscape is dotted with strange yet familiar structures. Stone staircases climb ten feet into the air and stop. Brick ledges hang in the sky, though nothing seems to be holding them up. Metal boxes are scattered all over the blue-green hills.

Mario hops onto a stack of red and blue cubes and snatches two shiny coins that are hanging above them. "These might come in handy later," he says. "I hear the princess just installed a new gumball machine at the palace." Then he continues on his way.

It usually takes Mario about thirty seconds to dash up the road to the palace. Today, though, it takes him almost ten minutes. Too many creatures get in his way.

He bounds up the grand marble staircase to the palace's front gate. One of the two royal doormen is standing guard. "Hello, Brock," Mario calls as he passes.

The muscular mushroom salutes, touching his furry white helmet.

Mario goes inside. As he walks down the main hall, he senses that all is not as it should be. Paintings are missing from the walls, and there are muddy footprints all over the royal carpets. Wooster, the king's finicky assistant, would never allow the palace to become such a mess—something must really be wrong!

Mario stops to inspect a pile of broken flower pots. Just then the other royal doorman walks by. "Hi, Gerkins," says Mario.

"I'm Brock," the doorman answers.

"Hmph," mutters Mario. "I thought I just saw Brock. Well, maybe I was wrong."

Mario hurries to the throne room. Along the way, he thinks he sees the same doorman a third time. Now he's confused. Maybe Princess Toadstool can clear up this mystery!

*** Mario collects two coins. ***
Turn to page 114.

40

Mario realizes that, in the Koopahari Desert, shortcuts aren't always a good idea. Sighing, he sets out along the main road.

After several hours of stomping Dry Bones, avoiding Fire Snakes, and sweating, he spots a sign by the road that reads, "FORT KOOPA 2,000 FEET (OR 10,000 TOES) AHEAD."

"It's about time," says Mario, trudging wearily along the sandy highway. "My feet are killing me." Ahead, the dark towers of Fort Koopa blot out the late afternoon sun.

Mario kneels to tighten his shoelace. As he does, he notices a tiny pebble in the road quivering like a Mexican jumping bean. Then larger stones begin to move. Soon, the whole ground around the plumber is shaking.

"I've got a feeling this isn't just a happy little earthquake," says Mario. He gazes down the road. Marching toward him are two enormous armored turtles.

"The Boomerang Brothers," he grumbles. "These guys always throw me some curves."

The last time Mario tangled with the Boomerang Brothers, he broke a tooth and ripped his best pair of red overalls. And that time, Luigi was there to help him.

"What's that?" rumbles one of the giant turtles, pointing to Mario. "An insect?"

"Hmmmmm," says the other one. "It could be a piece of sausage that fell off someone's pizza. Looks tasty."

Mario has no time to battle it out with the giant shell heads. He doubts he'd win if he did. This calls for strategy, not strength, so he waits until the massive creatures get dangerously close. Then he dashes between them and runs toward Fort Koopa.

"Come back here!" they howl in unison. "We're hungry!" Both turtles reach into giant holsters hanging at their sides and pull out handfuls of boomerangs. A cloud of deadly whirling objects screams after the plumber. If Mario can't dodge the weapons, he's through!

Solve this puzzle to find out what happens next:

• Choose any two of the giant turtles in this

drawing and follow the boomerang path from each of them to Mario.

• Add up the total number of boomerangs you encounter on the two trails.

• Add ten to your total if Mario has the extra power of the Super Mushroom to help him dodge the weapons.

If you've scored a total of 28 or higher,
turn to page 55.

If you've scored a total of 18 to 27, turn to
page 29.

If you've scored a total of 17 or less,
turn to page 28.

Roy hauls Mario onto the deck of the Doom Ship, smiling evilly the whole time. Behind him, Mario can see a tall, skinny man in green overalls tied to a mast.

"Luigi!" Mario cries. "How did you get up here? And who—"

"Good copy of your brother down there, wouldn't you agree?" Roy interrupts. "I'd tell you all about how we made it, but that would be a waste of my time." He dumps Mario, still tangled up in the vest, into a small metal cage. Then he drags the cage to the mouth of an enormous burlap bag.

"You should be flattered that we went through all this trouble just to get you two plumbers out of the way," Roy sneers. He shoves the cage into the bag and pushes Luigi in after it. Then, he ties the bag shut. Finally, he fastens a big yellow balloon to one end of the bag and pushes the whole thing overboard.

"What a drag," Mario complains to Luigi from deep inside the package. "My rescue plans are going down the drain."

"So long, suckers!" Roy leans back against a rusty Koopa cannon as Mario and Luigi drift helplessly off. "You'll never stop us now. The Koopas will rule the land!"

GAME OVER!

"Come back here, you rotten reptile," calls Mario, chasing after the Doom Ship.

As the evil boat begins to climb, Mario makes a jump for it. He snatches at a cluster of cables and wires hanging from the bottom of the vessel. Slowly, hand over hand, he climbs up to the wooden hull. There must be something solid to hold onto! At last, his fingers find a thin metal rail that encircles the boat's hull. He grabs it, throws one leg over, and hauls himself up.

Running a hand along the hull, Mario discovers a small hole with a cord dangling from it. He reels in the cord and finds an anchor tied to the end. That's useful!

He balances precariously on the thin rail. "Look, Ma! No hands!" he shouts. He swings the anchor around his head, hoping he can throw it onto the deck of the Doom Ship.

Solve this puzzle to see what happens next:

• Use a ruler or straight edge to draw a line in the direction that Mario's anchor is pointing.

• When the line reaches a new anchor, study it carefully. If it looks exactly like Mario's anchor, draw a line in the direction of the new anchor. Otherwise, continue drawing your line in the same direction until you come to another anchor.

• Repeat these steps. Eventually, you'll reach the top of the Doom Ship. Your line will lead you to directions that will tell you where to turn next.

If you land on the **O**, turn to page 94.

If you land on the **✖**, turn to page 105.

43

"Unhand my pal, you dirty weeds!" Mario shouts. He pushes his way through the growling green monsters.

One huge Piranha plant turns to face him. It runs a fleshy pink tongue across its lips and twists its green mouth into a horrible grin.

Mario picks up a baseball-sized rock and hurls it at the plant. "Batter up!" he calls.

Quickly, the creature picks up a large stick with its mouth and uses it to bat the stone away. Mario looks around. Oh no! Nearly all the Piranha plants have picked up sticks—and they're swinging them at him!

"Uh-oh," he mutters. "I shouldn't have given them any ideas."

The mean green sluggers block his path in every direction. Mario needs an exit, and fast!

Play this game to see what happens next:

• Start in the center of this drawing and move

two spaces in any direction to land on a box.

• Each time you land on a new space, read the number there and move that many spaces in the direction the arrow points.

• Keep moving until you land on a drawing of Mario or a Piranha plant. When that happens, the game is over. Look at the bottom of this page to find out where you should turn next.

↓ 1	↓ 1	↓ 1	→ 3	← 3	↓ 5	← 2
↓ 5	→ 3	← 1	→ 2	(Mario)	↑ 1	↓ 4
↓ 4	← 1	(plant)	↑ 2	→ 2	← 2	← 4
↑ 3	→ 1	↓ 1	START	↑ 2	→ 1	← 6
↓ 1	← 2	→ 4	→ 2	(plant)	↑ 2	↓ 2
→ 4	↑ 3	↑ 3	↑ 3	↑ 2	← 3	← 5
→ 1	(Mario)	→ 2	↑ 2	↑ 2	← 2	← 2

If you stop on a plant, turn to page 119.
If you stop on Mario, turn to page 78.

Mario takes his lucky penny out of his pocket and flings it at Iggy Koopa. "Heads I win, tails you lose," he shouts.

Ping! The coin knocks Iggy's glasses off his nose. "Hey! I can't see," squeals Iggy, fumbling for his spectacles. "No fair!"

Mario charges Iggy and gives him a hearty shove. Iggy skids across the floor, waving his arms helplessly until he crashes into a pile of books.

"One Koopa down," says Mario. Then someone taps him on the shoulder.

"Have some liquid, plumber!" shrieks a second Iggy Koopa. He heaves a test tube full of bubbling blue goo towards Mario. The plumber dives out of the way just in time as the vile liquid splashes onto the ground. With a hiss, a great patch of floor tiles vanish in a puff of blue smoke.

"Don't mess with draining fluid unless you

have a plumber's license," Mario advises Iggy II as he flings the phony turtle into a spool of wire.

A third Iggy attacks Mario, then a fourth. "This is ridiculous," Mario exclaims. "One Iggy is bad enough. Four is the worst!"

He fights the sand turtles off with his best jumps and kicks. He tries turning on a fan he finds in a corner, hoping to blow his opponents away. But whirling sand gets into the fan's engine and clogs it.

Each time Mario disposes of one Iggy, GLOM cranks out a new copy. Finally, the tenth Iggy sneaks up behind Mario and bashes him on the head with a telescope.

"I guess four Iggys aren't the worst," he thinks just before everything goes black.

A team of Iggy Koopas carries Mario back to the maze of mirrors and leaves him there. Mario dreams he's being trampled by thousands of Iggy Koopas dressed in business suits.

A few hours later he wakes up. "Oh, no, not the mirrors again," he moans. He gets to his feet, puts his cap on his aching head and marches toward where he thinks the lab is.

Turn to page 118.

Just then, Mario's foot slips. He teeters on the narrow rail for a few terrible seconds. Then he plunges toward the ground.

"Plumber overboard!" he shouts. Mario tries to grab one of the ropes trailing from the boat, but they all slip through his fingers. Fortunately, the Doom Ship has drifted away from the clusters of prickly Muncher plants. Mario plummets to the ground and lands in a moss garden with a thud.

Sitting up, he watches the sinister outline of the Doom Ship drift into the distance and disappear. "Oh, well. That's that," he says, brushing a few clumps of fuzzy green moss from his overalls. "The ride was making me seasick anyway."

He scampers back onto a nearby road and makes tracks for the Mushroom Kingdom.

Turn to page 58.

46

"My! This is a treat," exclaims a large turtle with a pink bow on her head. She sits on a pillow in the center of the room. "I had no idea Halloween came early this year."

It's Bowser's spoiled-rotten daughter. "Wendy O. Koopa!" groans Mario.

"That's me!" chirps another identical Wendy O. Koopa, stepping behind him.

"Me too," says a third turtle princess.

Mario whirls. Two more Wendy O. Koopas have shut the door behind him. "Going somewhere?" they ask in unison.

There must be at least a hundred Wendy O. Koopas in the room, though Mario has no time to count them. One by one, they leap forward to grab him. He dodges the first seven of them. Then the eighth Wendy knocks him down. He rolls to the side and gets back on his feet, but there's nowhere to run.

"What an ugly Halloween costume," twelve

Wendy O. Koopas chorus as they surround the terrified plumber.

The last thing Mario hears is a loudspeaker somewhere in the room, calling, "Two more Wendy O's, coming up!" Two new turtle princesses pop out from a large nozzle set into the floor.

More than fifty Wendy O. Koopas close in on Mario. Suddenly, everything goes black. Or is that pink?

GAME OVER!

Mario dives between two Firesnakes, rolls across a patch of sand, and then leaps over a third fiery beast. Several more whiz after him. He ducks just in time.

"Eat my dust, you crispy critters!" he shouts. Before any more Firesnakes can reach him, he throws himself behind the cluster of rocks at the far side of the ravine.

Mario leans against a rock for a few minutes until he catches his breath. "Whew!" he gasps. "That was hotter than Luigi's top secret spaghetti sauce."

Mario scouts along the ravine until at last he can see the walls of Fort Koopa. He jumps onto a stone and surveys the situation. "All I have to do is scale the fortress walls," he says. "No prob—"

Suddenly, something horrible flies directly at his head. It's a large black ball and chain—with fangs.

"Chain Chomp!" Mario yells. There's no time to duck. The thing's steel jaws close with a snap, only two inches from Mario's nose. Lucky for him, the monster is at the end of its leash. The heavy chain is bolted to a block set into the desert floor.

"I'm really having a ball now," mutters Mario. He wipes his forehead and wonders what to do next. Should he should try to dash past the Chain Chomp and scale the fortress walls? Or should he head back to the road?

Solve this puzzle for help:

• The blocks of bricks underneath the Chain Chomp follow a pattern. Study them carefully. Here's a hint: to find the truth, skip ahead and then step back.

• Look at the four blocks below the drawing and try to guess which one should go next in the series.

• Follow the directions after your choice to cross out some of the links in the Chain Chomp's chain. The letters in the remaining links will tell you what Mario should do next.

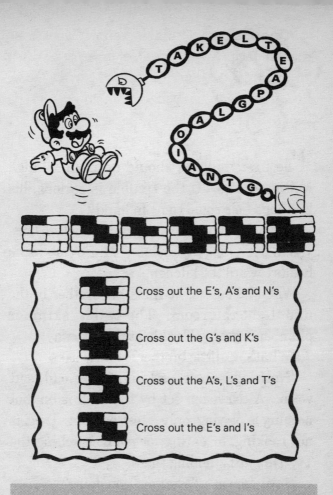

Cross out the E's, A's and N's

Cross out the G's and K's

Cross out the A's, L's and T's

Cross out the E's and I's

If you think Mario should try to get past the Chain Chomp, turn to page 40.

If you think Mario should go back to the main road, turn to page 81.

48

The first thing he should do is find Luigi, Mario decides. If the trouble is serious, his brother's help could come in handy.

"If you're having a midnight snack, I hope you're not eating my cookies," Mario calls as he heads toward the kitchen.

When he enters, he finds his brother in the middle of the room. The taller, skinnier plumber is gazing blankly at the doorway.

"What's up, little brother?" Mario asks.

"Nothing," answers Luigi in an odd, soft voice. A television set by the sink is on, but nothing is playing, only a test pattern. Luigi is not cooking, or eating, or even watching the TV. He's just standing there.

Mario frowns. "What are you doing?"

"Waiting for you," Luigi mumbles. He walks through the kitchen, heading for the shop. Then he slowly turns and beckons to Mario. "Now that you're here, there's something I'd like to show you," he says in a weird, flat voice. "Come see my new invention—a flying machine."

Mario pauses, wondering what to do.

Solve this puzzle to help decide what Mario should do next:

• The box above Mario's head contains a secret message. If you can read it, it will give you a clue.

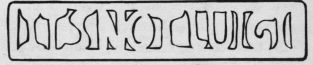

If you think Mario should go outside with Luigi, turn to page 71.

If you think Mario should leave him and head to the Mushroom Kingdom, turn to page 25.

49

Mario steps onto the brick road that winds through the Mushroom Kingdom. Immediately, a bright blue snapping turtle charges at him. Mario hops into the air. The small reptile scuttles underneath without touching him.

"Those Koopa Troopas aren't very bright," Mario says, watching the turtle scamper off.

Just then, he feels something bump into him and a sharp pain shoots through his leg. He looks down to find another turtle with its teeth dug into his ankle.

"Ouch! Where did you come from?" asks Mario, picking up the small blue turtle. It looks exactly like the one he just dodged.

Mario frowns at the turtle, but it doesn't answer. "Oh, never mind," he says. He drops it to the ground and shoves it out of the way.

"Things seem normal enough," he notes as he looks about the countryside. But after a minute he begins to change his mind.

The Mushroom Kingdom is made up of open meadows, rolling hills, and valleys. There's usually room for every creature there to go about its business undisturbed. But today, for some reason, the kingdom seems crowded. Beetles swarm about in such great numbers that a single flock entirely covers a grassy hill by the road. Orange Tweeter birds fight for space on a nearby brick ledge.

Mario watches two tiny masked creatures walk by. That's strange, too, he thinks. Shyguys almost always travel alone.

"I'd better get to the bottom of this," says Mario, gazing around. A few feet ahead, the road forks. One path zig-zags up to the royal palace. The other winds around some metal boxes and fades into the distance.

Mario must decide which path to take. He's sure he'll find trouble on either one.

If you think Mario should go to the palace, turn to page 79.

If you think Mario should explore the Mushroom Kingdom, turn to page 26.

Mario frantically tries to pick the Micro-Goombas off his overalls, but there are just too many of them. When a new batch drops from the sky, the heroic plumber stumbles and falls. Soon he's buried under a blanket of baby mushrooms. Slowly, the sweet odor of Goomba gas sends Mario into a deep sleep.

Two big Para-Goombas swoop down toward him. One pecks at an exposed part of Mario's arm.

"Icky, icky, blech!" the beast squawks.

The Para-Goombas decide they'd rather not eat the unconscious plumber after all. They fly off, taking their babies with them.

When Mario wakes, he can't remember a thing that just happened. The Goomba gas has made him forget everything. He rubs the sleep from his eyes and wanders back to the entrance of the Mushroom Kingdom.

Turn to page 102.

Mario whirls the anchor over his head a few times. Then he lets it go. It soars up to the deck of the Doom Ship and hooks neatly into one of the wooden floorboards.

"Yeee-ha!" hollers Mario, as he swings up the rope. But when he lands feet first on the deck, he finds more than he expected.

Roy is there, scraping his dirty toenails against the ship's warped floorboards. And behind Roy, a tall, skinny plumber in green overalls is gagged and tied to the main mast. It's Luigi!

"Roy, it's illegal to steal people's brothers," says Mario. "Give Luigi back now, and I promise I'll only beat you to a pulp."

"Oh yeah? You and what army?" cries Roy. He stomps forward.

"Don't worry, I'll bring you flowers when you're in the hospital," Mario goes on.

"Oh, yeah?" The furious turtle's huge, yellow teeth are now inches from Mario's face. He swings his paw. Mario ducks.

"You missed," Mario says. "Would you like to try again, or do you want to surrender now?"

"Rrooaarr!" Roy hurls himself at Mario.

Play this game to find out what happens when Roy charges at Mario:

• Choose one of the three shapes in the space above the word "START."

• Read the number in the shape you chose and move that many spaces along the track. Repeat this when you reach a new space. Keep the same shape every time.

• If you stop on a space where your shape has an X in it, follow the arrow and read the message it points to. The message will tell you where to turn next.

If you land on the ✳, turn to page 8.

If you land on the ✱, turn to page 44.

Mario walks on, glancing left and right at his reflection. Distracted by the presence of so many good-looking plumbers, he slams face-first into a wall of glass.

"Ouch," he mutters, rubbing his nose. "I wish Luigi were here. Then I could make him lead the way."

The mirrored path bends to the left. Winking at the plumber on his right, he turns left and walks ahead for a few feet. Again, he runs headlong into a clear glass wall. "Whoever cleans this glass can do my shop windows anytime," he says to himself.

Using his head as a compass, Mario moves through the maze for what seems like hours, but all he gets for his trouble is a colossal headache. At last he comes to a branch in the maze with two ways to go—left or right. The problem is, he isn't sure he hasn't been this way before.

"All right," he says. "I've had enough. There must be some way out of this place."

If Mario has the hammer, turn to page 73.

If you think Mario should go right, turn to page 60.

If you think Mario should go left, turn to page 16.

A fiery streak zips past Mario's face, scorching his mustache. Then another Firesnake slices into his shoe.

"Ow! My toes!" cries Mario, backing away from the two fire-monsters. He stops when a searing pain in his foot tells him he has just stepped on a whole nest of them.

"Yeow!" he shouts. "I can't beat the heat— I'm heading back to the road!"

Mario hurries back the way he came. Looking over his shoulder, he sees a crowd of Firesnakes in the ravine below.

"That's just too hot to handle!" he pants.

*** If Mario had a Super Mushroom, he dropped it while running from the Firesnakes — it's gone! ***

Turn to page 81.

"Sorry, little brother, I've got to reach Fort Koopa," says Mario. "I'm sure you can take care of your double by yourself."

"Wish me luck," says Luigi. He leans over the rail and gives his brother the secret plumber's handshake. Then he slides down a rope and drops to the ground.

Mario walks over to the steering wheel and inspects the buttons on the control panel. "Now, how do I make this crate go to Fort Koopa?"

He locates a large blue switch marked, "Return to Sender," and flips it on. Instantly, the Doom Ship lurches forward, cruising through the sky at top speed.

"That should do it," says Mario. He leans against a mast and lets the boat guide itself through the desert skies.

All of a sudden, a terrible odor wafts over the side of the ship. "I'd know that smell anywhere," says Mario, holding his nose. "We're at Fort Koopa."

He peers over the rail. Sure enough, he is now hovering over the sooty stone fortress that the Koopas use as their summer home.

He scrambles down a rope and walks up to the front gate. No one is there. Mario thinks about calling out "Yoo-hoo! Anyone home?" but he decides to let himself in quietly instead.

He sneaks through the hallways. There seems to be no one there but himself—and several hundred piles of soot.

"I've heard of dust bunnies before, but these must be dust buffaloes!" Mario says, kicking aside great piles of fuzz. He wanders through the filthy halls of Fort Koopa until he rounds a corner. Suddenly he runs smack into a large, leathery knee.

"Hi and goodbye!" a raspy voice snarls.

Mario is in the Koopa throne room—at the feet of King Bowser Koopa himself.

"Oops! Wrong address," Mario says. But it's too late for him to back out.

Turn to page 12.

Snap! The vicious Chain Chomp sinks its teeth into Mario's big toe.

"Yeow!" he shouts. He falls off the wall and tumbles to the ground. The monster snaps again. It misses only because Mario is jumping up and down, holding his foot in pain.

"I'd better retreat while I still have feet!" wails Mario, hopping away from the wall.

The Chain Chomp continues snapping until Mario is well out of range. Then it settles down in its nest to snack on the tasty piece of leather from Mario's shoe.

Limping, Mario heads out of the ravine.

Turn to page 81.

"Thank goodness you're here," cries Princess Toadstool the moment Mario opens the royal double doors. She's dressed in a long pink evening gown and matching earrings. She's as beautiful as ever, Mario thinks. But her finger-nails are bitten all the way to the quick. She looks really stressed out!

"I was afraid you didn't get my message," she says, fingering her gold and emerald necklace.

Mario gazes around the throne room. The place is a madhouse. There are two of almost everyone in the hall! Everyone is yelling at his or her double. Even one of the royal pool clean-ers is looking in a mirror and yelling at her reflection. "I guess she got confused," Princess Toadstool says.

"Looks like you've got a major disaster on your hands, Princess," says Mario. "But what happened?"

"It all started two days ago, when the mailman showed up with bunches of flowers for everyone," explains Princess Toadstool. "Everyone took the flowers to their room. But Wooster dropped his, Toad's, and mine when I asked him to put them on the windowsill. Then the next morning when Wooster watered the king's flowers, they started crackling and shooting sparks. All the bouquets had strange-looking tiny video cameras hidden in them!"

The princess's heels click on the throne room's marble floor as she paces anxiously. "As soon as we figured that out, we threw all the flowers away. But it was too late. Doubles of almost everyone began to appear. Since then, things have been getting more and more confusing. No one can remember whom they've spoken to, the royal refrigerator is empty from feeding all the extras, and swarms of monsters are overrunning the kingdom!"

Mario arches one bushy black eyebrow. "I smell a big, fat Koopa rat," he says.

"That's not the worst part," warns the princess, adjusting her tiny crown. . . .

Turn to page 53.

Mario's plumber's pockets are chockful of useful stuff, but no magnifying glass.

"Time to look for Toad!" Mario declares. Promising the princess he'll be back as soon as possible, he rushes out of the palace and heads off into the Mushroom Kingdom. As he skips down a hill, he trips over a large metal pipe-stump. "What's this?" he says, peering into the circular opening. Below him, a small, dimly-lit chamber is filled with sparkling coins. It's also sprinkled with Shyguys.

"Yahoo!" shouts Mario, diving into the pit. He gathers as many coins as he can before climbing back out onto the grass.

"This is great," he says, counting his change. "Now I can buy Luigi that electric bowling ball he's been asking for." He drops the coins into one of his overalls pockets and continues his search for Toad.

Solve this puzzle to find out how many coins Mario collects:

- Study this map carefully.
- Cross out any three Shyguy pests.
- Count up the total number of coins that Mario will be able to reach without touching any of the remaining Shyguys. Mario may follow more than one path to collect coins, but don't count any coin more than once!

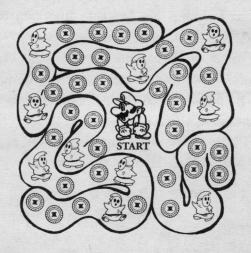

START

If Mario gathered 20 or more coins, turn to page 55.

If Mario gathered fewer than 20 coins, turn to page 21.

58

"Here goes nothing," Mario mutters as he turns left and walks past several rows of mirrors. Then he goes right for a few feet. Then he turns back and goes left again. Finally he stops and shakes his head, feeling very confused. "Help!" he wails. "I'm lost!"

He takes off his cap and scratches his head. He paces around in circles for a few minutes. Then he walks on to the next dividing point and takes out the coin again. "Let's see. This time I'll go right if it's heads, and left if it's tails," Mario says. He flips the coin.

Flip a penny to decide where Mario should go next:

HEADS, turn to page 60.

TAILS, turn to page 16.

59

A weedy-looking Piranha plant swings its bat. Mario jumps straight up into the air. "Strike one!" he yells.

But the play is better than a strike. Instead of hitting the plumber, the bat squelches into the pulpy flesh of another plant. The injured plant howls and swings back. *Ska-Blump!* Its bat smashes into a third one. The Piranha Patch soon becomes a field of furious green sluggers. The monster plants forget all about Mario as they bash each other.

"Psst! Toad, come on!" whispers Mario. Toad crawls out from his hiding place and he and Mario tiptoe out of the patch unnoticed.

"Shall we strike out for the palace, little buddy?" asks Mario once they're on safe ground. He jumps up and snatches a coin from a nearby ledge.

"You bet!" Toad says. As they make their way home, he hands Mario a magnifying glass.

"Here's what I was looking for."

Mario winks. "This'll be a hit."

Soon they're back in the throne room.

*** Mario collects one coin, and he now has the magnifying glass. ***

Turn to page 64.

Drip by Drip Scorecard

Circle each object as you collect it.

Keep track of your coins here:

Now, use this chart to find out how good a plumber you are. Count up the total number of coins that Mario collected during his adventure. Score 10 points for each coin. Then look up your rating on the chart.

Did Mario rescue Luigi? Did he help fight Luigi's double? Did he get past the Firesnakes and the Chain Chomp? Read the book again, until you get the best possible score.

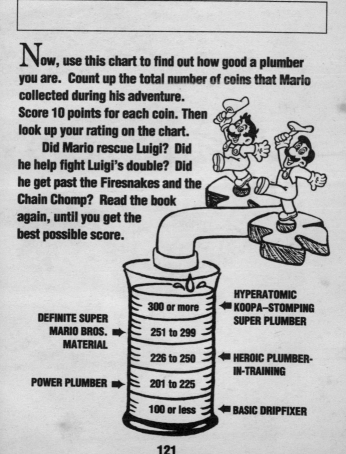

HYPERATOMIC
KOOPA–STOMPING
SUPER PLUMBER

300 or more

DEFINITE SUPER
MARIO BROS.
MATERIAL

251 to 299

226 to 250 ← HEROIC PLUMBER-
IN-TRAINING

POWER PLUMBER

201 to 225

100 or less ← BASIC DRIPFIXER